# Grandmother's Happy Poems For Children

### by
### Julia Winter Cohen

To Allie,
Reach for the stars,
Love from Grandma & Grandpa,
Lovingly,
Grandmother Julia

### Illustrated by
### Christopher Gerlach

# C. E. Winter Publishing
# Santa Fe

*535 Cordova Rd.*
*Suite 111*
*Santa Fe, NM 87501*

Text copyright © 1997 Julia Winter Cohen
Illustration copyright © 1997 Christopher S. Gerlach

NO REPRODUCTION OF THIS BOOK OR IT'S
ILLUSTRATION IS ALLOWED WITHOUT PERMISSION IN
WRITING FROM THE PUBLISHER

PRINTED IN THE UNITED STATES OF AMERICA
RECYCLED PAPER AND SOY INK
WERE USED IN THIS WORK

Cohen, Julia Winter.
    Grandmother's happy poems for children / by Julia Winter Cohen; illustrated by Christopher Gerlach.
    p. cm.
    Preassigned LCCN: 96-61376
    SUMMARY: Spiritual, non-denominational guidance for children and families, with an emphasis on values, faith and positive living.
    ISBN 0-9654713-0-6

1. Spiritual life-Juvenile poetry.   I. Title.
PS3553.O446G73 1996       811'.54
                                  QBI96-2570

*This little book is dedicated
with love to my grandchildren
Julianne
Wendy
Eric Carl
and
Scott
and for the pleasure of
children
everywhere.*

# Table of Contents

The First of May ............................................... 1
Going to School ............................................... 2
God is in You ................................................... 3
It's Raining ...................................................... 4
God is with Me ................................................. 6
Across the Ocean ............................................. 7
Long Ago ......................................................... 8
Life Song ......................................................... 9
The Apple Tree ............................................... 10
A Little Worm ................................................. 12
Flowers ........................................................... 13
My Dog ........................................................... 14
God Directs Me .............................................. 16
Pitter Patter .................................................... 17
Seasons ........................................................... 18
Imagination .................................................... 19
Boys and Girls ................................................ 20
The Giraffe ..................................................... 22
I Am Fine ........................................................ 23
My Prayer ....................................................... 24
Me ................................................................... 26
Dreams ............................................................ 27
In The Sky ...................................................... 28
Eating .............................................................. 29
Life .................................................................. 30
Trust ................................................................ 31
Dear God ......................................................... 32
God .................................................................. 34
Write your own poems .................................... 35

# List of Color Illustrations

The Day Looks Gloomy ............................... 5

Mother, Here I Am ......................................... 11

My Dog And I Take Long Walks ................. 15

Whenever I'm Blue ........................................ 25

Dear God ........................................................ 33

## THE FIRST OF MAY

The river runs deep through the forest,
The sun shines bright on the hill,
And sitting on the branch of a leafy tree
Warbles the whippoorwill.

Spring is with us again,
Summer is on the way;
Sing and be happy,
It's the first of May.

## GOING TO SCHOOL

When I go to school
Each day,
I say a prayer
Along the way.

I thank God
For His constant care,
For being with me
Everywhere.

Whether at home
Or play or at school,
God's way is that
Of the Golden Rule.

Which means
To everyone be kind,
Then true Happiness
You will find.

# GOD IS IN YOU

Mother, where is God?
I would like to know.
Is he in my dog, Cappy,
And the pretty flowers that grow?

Is He in the ocean?
And the sunshine too?
In the big cat next door?
And in me and you?

If God is in all of this
And everything you say,
How do you describe Him
In a very simple way?

If God is in all of us,
And is good as you say,
Then He is the one
Who brings happiness our way.

# IT'S RAINING

The day looks gloomy
From the inside out,
Oh, it is raining
Without a doubt.

But what is
That to me?
God made the rain
To set nature free.

The rain helps
The flowers to grow,
Soon their beautiful
Blossoms will show.

To brighten the earth
With all their glory,
Then it will be
Another story.

The day looks gloomy

## **GOD IS WITH ME**

Dear God, now I'm tucked in bed,
I'm a little sleepy head.
My Mom will soon turn out the light,
And she'll be out of sight.

But I know that You are there.
I'm always in Your tender care.
You are with me night and day,
Guiding in Your wondrous way.

Make me Loving,
Kind and True,
Thank you God
For all You do.

## ACROSS THE OCEAN

Across the ocean deep and wide,
Children live on the other side.

They play like me and go to school,
And I hope follow the Golden Rule.

Which means be kind to one another,
And always treat each one as a sister
or a brother.

## LONG AGO

Long ago people thought
The world was flat.
We now know that it isn't,
What do you think of that?

Long ago people thought
The moon was made of green cheese.
We now know that it isn't,
Men have walked on it, if you please.

Long ago people thought
Man would never fly.
But now airplanes
Are up there in the sky.

Long ago people thought
God was way far up above.
But now we know God is in us,
He is our life and He is love.

## LIFE SONG

There is one God,
There is one Heart
To which we all belong.
If we would realize this
Life could be a song.

There would be one melody
For everyone to sing;
As all harmonized,
Joy and happiness
It would bring.

# THE APPLE TREE

Mother, here I am
Up in the apple tree.
There are lots of apples
Here for you and me.

There are one,
two, three, four,
Too many apples
For me to count
On this apple tree.

If we are God's children,
How can He keep count
Of every variety,
And such a large amount?

Oh, you say,
He knows each one,
All are in His care,
Because at the center
Of each one,
God is there.

Mother, here I am

## A LITTLE WORM

Playing in the yard today,
I found a little worm.

He looked like a thick string,
And how that worm did squirm.

He wriggled and he waggled
As he went along his way.

I know he was saying,
"I'm alive, hurrah!"

## FLOWERS

Bluebells are blue,
And pinks are pink;
And pansies come in
All colors, I think.

One thing I know
God makes them grow,
And I enjoy them so,
There in a row.

## MY DOG

My dog and I take long walks,
And we have very many talks.
I tell him all about my dreams,
About how big I'll be some day.
And then, I'll have to go away
To study life and history,
So life won't be such a mystery.
Then I'll travel far and wide,
With him always at my side.
For in all the world there couldn't be
A better pal than he.

My dog and I take long walks

## GOD DIRECTS ME

God guards and guides me
Day by day,
In His most wondrous way.
If I listen to God's voice,
It isn't for me to make a choice.
I know the right thing to do,
For God directs
And sees me through.

## PITTER - PATTER

Listen to the pitter-patter of the rain,
Tapping on the window pane.
Little droplets from the sky,
Stopping by to say, "Hi!
Better stay inside and play.
Outside is NOT for you today."

## SEASONS

How I like to skip and run,
In the warm Springtime sun.
Summer comes,
And it gets hot,
Then I go to our swimming spot.
In the Fall
The skating's great,
But I can hardly wait
For the Winter snow,
When on my sled
I can go.
The Seasons come one by one,
So that I can have
Different kinds of fun.
God did this for you and me,
And is all loving
As you can see.

# IMAGINATION

I am just a little child
With an imagination
That does
Run wild.

I can be a bear
Rubbing its back
On a tree.
My mind
Sets the stage for me.

I like to pretend
I am a little dog,
Or a horse
As I jog.

I can be a grown-up
Like Mom or Dad,
Or a baby
Lying on a pad.

I can fly
Up in a tree,
And sing like a bird
Tweet, tweet, twee.

There's no limit
To what I can be,
My mind
Sets the stage for me.

## BOYS AND GIRLS

Little girls
And little boys
Like to play
With a lot of toys.

There is the drum
With its tum! tum! tum!
And balls and bats,
And funny hats.

There are dolls
And jacks
And marbles too,
So very many things to do.

They like to jump
They want to run.
Keep busy
And have fun.

Companionship and love
Are what they need
No question
Of race or creed.

Children love
One another,
As do
Sister and brother.

## THE GIRAFFE

Baby Giraffe
With your wobbly knees,
Standing next to your mother
In perfect ease.
She is so tall
With her neck so long;
You will be that big
When you are grown and strong.
You will look down
On the crowds
As they go by
With the same critical eye.

# I AM FINE

When I'm at play and stub my toe,
I may cry with pain.
But I know God's there
And I'll be fine again.

He is the One who is within,
Who is my Life and Soul.
God is the One who made me
And keeps me well and whole.

# MY PRAYER

Whenever I'm blue
And don't know what to do;
I think of You God,
I think of You.

I pray to You
In my humble way,
And I know You answer
For I hear You say . . .

"Be still and know that
I care for you,
You are My child
I'll see you through.

I will guide you
Day by day
If you but take
The time to pray."

Whenever I'm blue

# **ME**

My spirit within
Is calling to God
To assure me I'm not
Just earth and sod.

# DREAMS

I am a child of God.
He is deep inside,
The one in whom I can confide.
All the dreams I see,
Through God, can come to me.
For when I do the work
I should do,
He will do the rest
To see me through.
Whenever I succeed
I know God
Fullfilled my need.

## IN THE SKY

When I'm way up in the sky
And look on the roads below,
They look like little ribbons
Running to and fro.
The cars are
Oh so small,
You hardly see them at all.

When the drivers look at the sky,
And see a plane up so high,
They wonder who's inside
Going for that fast ride.
I can't see them,
They can't see me,
But I know I'm here,
Happy as can be.

# EATING

We eat in the morning,
At noon and at night.
At times it is
A great delight.
At other times
It's quite a bore.
We can't wait
To get out the door.

It's time to go to school,
To swim or play,
And having to eat gets in the way.
But, it is a thing
We have to do,
To grow strong and healthy too.
So I'll eat and thankful be,
That good food is here for me.

## LIFE

All the birds and the bees,
The apples upon the trees,
The dogs, the cats,
The cow, the deer,
All declare
That God is here.
For God is life
Expressing through
Everything we see and do.
And that means — me and you, too.

# TRUST

Dear God,
I'm just a little child
In this world
So big and wide.
But I won't ever be afraid,
Because I know You are my Guide.
I know You are with me always,
No matter where I go.
I just trust in You,
And the right path You will show.

# DEAR GOD

Dear God,
I thank You for this day,
I thank You for Your power,
I thank You for Your protecting Love
That encircles me hour by hour.

You are always with me
No matter how life's road may bend,
I know that I can count on You,
My God, and my Dearest Friend.

Dear God

# GOD

God of Light,
God of Might,
I am always
In Thy sight

You are deep
Within my soul,
This I know,
And am made whole.

Whole, complete,
My strength's in You,
You are my Life
And will guide me through.

Dear Girls and Boys

Now that you have read my poems, why not write some of your own. These blank pages are for you.

      Love,
      Grandmother Julia

A place for more of your poems ............

And some more of your poems ............

ABOUT THE AUTHOR: *Julia Winter Cohen was raised in the Midwest. She moved to California with her family in the 1930's, and lived in Los Angeles for many years. She now lives in Santa Fe, New Mexico. She is the much beloved mother and grandmother of two daughters and four grandchildren. Over the years, she continued to write these "gifts of love" and now has decided to share them with children everywhere. They come from her own vision of the Divine, whom she calls God. She continues to write, to lavish love on her family, and to receive it equally in return. This book, Grandmother's Happy Poems For Children is her first sharing in print of her special expression of her love of life.*

ABOUT THE ILLUSTRATOR: *Christopher S. Gerlach was born in Wareham, Massachusetts, grew up there and in the Western United States. He has followed a creative star for most of his life, enjoying drawing, painting, music, poetry, and the dance of life in all its beautiful forms. He spent many years abroad painting and traveling. On returning to the United States he has lived in many places that mingle light and natural beauty, most recently the mountains of southwestern Colorado. He has painted and exhibited landscapes in many places, and has loved publishing and sharing in print all his life.*